Dear Parents,

Welcome to the Scholastic Reader series. We have taken over 80 years of experience with teachers, parents, and children and put it into a program that is designed to match your child's interests and skills.

Level 1—Short sentences and stories made up of words kids can sound out using their phonics skills and words that are important to remember.

Level 2—Longer sentences and stories with words kids need to know and new "big" words that they will want to know.

Level 3—From sentences to paragraphs to longer stories, these books have large "chunks" of texts and are made up of a rich vocabulary.

Level 4—First chapter books with more words and fewer pictures.

It is important that children learn to read well enough to succeed in school and beyond. Here are ideas for reading this book with your child:

- Look at the book together. Encourage your child to read the title and make a prediction about the story.
- Read the book together. Encourage your child to sound out words when appropriate. When your child struggles, you can help by providing the word.
- Encourage your child to retell the story. This is a great way to check for comprehension.
- Have your child take the fluency test on the last page to check progress.

Scholastic Readers are designed to support your child's efforts to learn how to read at every age and every stage. Enjoy helping your child learn to read and love to read.

> —**Francie Alexander**
> Chief Education Officer
> Scholastic Education

For Andrew and Peter,
who like to stay put
—S.K.

For Jack, my big brother
—L.D.

Text copyright © 1998 by Stephen Krensky.
Illustrations copyright © 1998 by Larry DiFiori.
Activities copyright © 2003 Scholastic Inc.

All rights reserved. Published by Scholastic Inc.
SCHOLASTIC, CARTWHEEL BOOKS, and associated logos are trademarks
and/or registered trademarks of Scholastic Inc.

Library of Congress Cataloging-in-Publication Data is available.

ISBN 0-590-33127-2

22 21 20 19   11 12 13 14/0

Printed in the U.S.A.   40
First printing, February 1998

We Just MOVED!

by Stephen Krensky
Illustrated by Larry DiFiori

Scholastic Reader — Level 2

SCHOLASTIC INC.
New York Toronto London Auckland Sydney
Mexico City New Delhi Hong Kong Buenos Aires

We just moved out of our house.

It was a big job.
We packed all our clothing.

We loaded all our furniture.

And we took our pets, too.

The trip took a while.
We got stuck in a lot of traffic.

Our new place is bigger
than our old place.

It was dark when we arrived.
I heard a strange noise.

My parents said it was just the wind.

In the morning I looked out.
My room has a nice view.

It took a while to explore everything.
There is a modern kitchen.

We found a playroom in the basement.

Some of the new neighbors
looked in on us right away.
They seem very friendly.

But I haven't made up my mind
about everyone.

There's a town nearby.
I'm learning my way around.
Some of the stores look like the ones
where I used to live.

People do some things differently here.

But they do some things the same.

The kids here have different rules
for their games.
But I'm getting used to them.

Of course, I still miss my old friends.
I like hearing from them.

The more time I spend here,
the more comfortable I get.

It's starting to feel like home.

31901050920331